TEYLA KAI'S ADVENTURES
THE LOST WINGS

The life of a fairy is not easy when you're a kid. Wand lessons and practice are a huge portion of my life.

Sometimes I wish I wasn't a fairy...

One day, while practicing with her wand, Teyla Kai saw Rachel. Rachel is the human girl that lives in the big brown house. She's always playing with her mom and dad, helping them in the garden, and eating ice cream! Being a fairy is so boring! thought Teyla Kai. So much responsibility to practice my magic. Sometimes I wish I was a human!

TEYLA KAI'S ADVENTURES

THE LOST WINGS

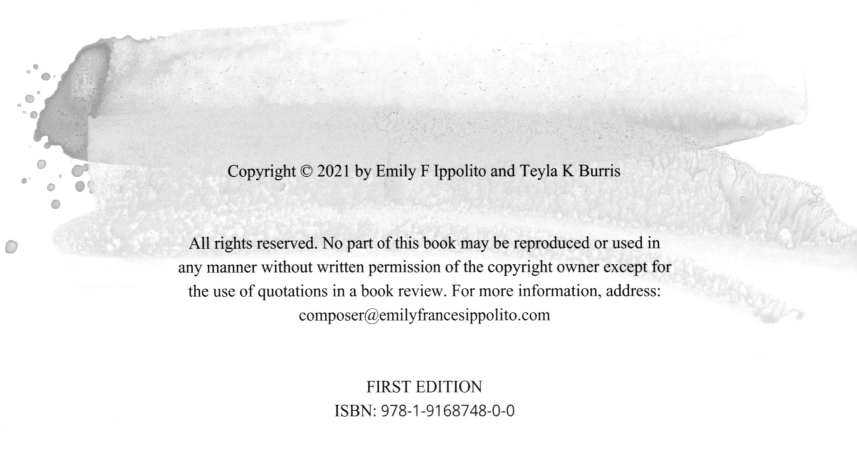

FIRST EDITION
ISBN: 978-1-9168748-0-0

www.emilyfrancesippolito.com

Just then, a strong gust of wind swept up Teyla Kai's wand and tossed it far far away.

Teyla Kai flew after the wand and found it next to the shiniest penny she had ever seen. It wasn't like your usual penny, it was shining so bright as if there was a light from inside.

The light flickered and danced, mesmerizing Teyla Kai. She took a closer look and saw there were words that seemed to be an instruction of how to use its magic.

Teyla Kai started to read the poem aloud:

"Wandering minds, near and far, hold this penny close, make a wish of what you want, with a zoom and a swoosh"

"Wandering minds,
near and far,
hold this penny close,
make a wish of
what you want,
with a zoom and
a swoosh"

Teyla Kai wanted to be a human more than anything! So she zoomed around yelling at the top of her lungs as she flew! "I want to be a human!". Nothing happened...

Then she tried swooshing her wand from side to side. The clouds parted with a ray of sun on her face. Surely, this was the magic happening! She waited and waited in this warm stream of sunlight.. Nothing...

Finally, Teyla Kai decided she must have to hold the penny close. She struggled to hold the huge, human size penny. She managed to push the penny like a wheel along the grass and leaned it against a tree to help with the weight of the heavy penny.

She stood in front of this huge penny and wished with all her heart to be human.

Just then another gust of wind swooshed her right off of her feet and zoomed her into the wind again! She lost control of her wings and started to feel very strange. She was terribly worried and didn't know what to do! Her wings started to disappear and she began to grow and grow and grow!!! She was on her way to becoming a human!

Teyla Kai's dream of being a human was finally coming true! However, instead of feeling excited, she soon became scared. It felt too strange to be a human. She had long legs that fumbled over each other as she tried to walk.

She had long dangly arms that felt as if she could touch the sky, which made her afraid she was going to hit into everything! Frightened and panicked, she ran as fast as she could. She didn't know where to run, but just kept running and running and running. She had to figure out how to turn back into a fairy! She could hear the laughter of children as she ran. She ran and ran until she reached the park. So many times she wished she could experience what it was like to play in this park.

Just then she heard the pitter patter of feet. It was Rachel, the human girl she would watch and admire. Frightened, Teyla Kai quietly stood there. She was so panicked inside about becoming a human and didn't want Rachel to know what had happened. At the same time she was so excited to finally be able to talk to Rachel instead of just watching her. "Hi", Rachel said. "Do you want to play with me?". Teyla Kai said "Sure, I would love to play! Then the girls ran and played all sorts of games, like tag, hop scotch, and hide and seek.

It was such a dream for Teyla Kai to play all of these human games that she nearly forgot how scared she was. The time seemed to fly by. The sun began to disappear as the day was soon to become night. Teyla Kai was worried that the other fairies were looking for her. She had been on such a long adventure, she was sure the other fairies would not believe her. What was she going to do? How was she going to get back to the other fairies? Most importantly, how was she going to become a fairy again?

She decided to tell Rachel what had happened, but Rachel seemed to think it was a very detailed play time story. Teyla Kai continued to play, swinging on the swings and going down the slide.

As she flew down the slide she noticed a sparkling light in the distance. She ran towards the light and next to a bush was her wand. She hadn't even noticed she had dropped it! Next to her wand was the same penny. But how did that huge penny get all the way over here? She hadn't moved it away from the tree. This time the penny felt light and small. As a human you could lift big objects just with your fingers! She flipped around the penny to see the back of it.

There was a finger print on the penny but with a closer look had words that said:

"Place your finger right here, for you will know when it's time. Then throw the penny in the air, for another to find."

She tried to explain to Rachel how this was a magical penny. She described her whole adventure from beginning to end and told Rachel that if she did what the back of the penny said, she was likely going to turn back into a fairy again. Rachel, who still didn't believe her, played along with this "story" and hugged Teyla goodbye.

Teyla Kai placed her finger on the penny and then threw it in the air. A swoosh of wind came and a swirl of leaves danced around Teyla Kai's feet. To Rachel's disbelief Teyla Kai got smaller, and smaller, and smaller! Teyla Kai had turned back into a fairy! Both girls couldn't wait to tell their families of their adventures, although Rachel's parents chuckled at her story. It would always be a friendship and story that was near and dear to her heart! Teyla Kai now had a human friend but would never doubt how wonderful it was to just be herself again.

THE END

Meet The Illustrator

Khaled Ibn Anwar

"Hi! I'm Khaled, professional digital artist and illustrator. I enjoy colorful and detailed art styles and love to play with colors. It was an exciting opportunity for me to illustrate this fantastic story."

Khaled has many years of experience in painting and sketching. He specializes in digital and concept art in addition to illustration. He currently resides in Bangladesh and hopes to work with people from all around the world to help bring their imagination to life.

To see more of Khaled's amazing artwork check out his website: kia_artbox.artstation.com

To contact Khaled for hire please email him at kianwar71@gmail.com

Dedicated to all
those with a child-
like heart and a
sense of wonder.
Always dream big
and stay true to
yourself because you
are special just the
way you are!

Thank you for following Teyla Kai on her first adventure! Stay tuned for future publications of Teyla Kai's continued adventures.

Arwen,

   Dream big, Laugh loud, and let
   your inner magic shine!

Thank you,

Emily Appleton & Teyla Kai

24/05/24